A Birthday for Danny's Bee

written and photographed
by
Mia Coulton

I have a toy
named Bee.

Today is Bee's birthday.

3 6109 00388 3904

3

"I have a little birthday hat for you," said Danny.
"I have a big birthday hat for me."

"I have a little birthday cake for you," said Danny.

"Look, Bee!" said Danny.

"I have a little birthday card for you.

I made it just for you."

"This box

is for you, too!"

Danny said.

"Look inside

the box, Bee."

"Now you have a little toy Danny!" said Danny.